It starts with 1 line.

Happy Reading!

I dedicate this story to my family,

who has always supported my creativity.

One day a BLUE line named Royal, was kicking his ball at the park. He was hoping another blue line would come along and play with him.

Royal turned around and was surprised to see a GREEN, curved, line.

Royal had NEVER seen a green, curved line before.

"Hi! I'm Royal. Who are you?"

The Green, curved line smiled, "Hi! I'm Leif. I just moved here."

Royal looked at Leif from head to toe.

Leif looked at himself, confused, and said, "Is there something wrong?"

"Have you always been Green and curved?" Royal asked.

Leif laughed," Of course I have."

Leif looked Royal up and down. "Have you always been Blue and long?" Leif asked.

"Yes," Royal answered shyly, "I've never met another colour or different line before."

Royal had an idea, "Do you want to play ball with me?"

"I'd love to!" Leif exclaimed.

Royal and Leif kicked the ball back and forth until another line appeared. This line was different then either one of them.

This line was RED and a GIRL!!!

"Hi! I'm Cherry."

She said with a smile. "Can I play with you guys?"

Royal and Leif looked at Cherry.

"But you're a girl?" Royal stated.

"AND?" Cherry answered stepping back.

"Girls don't usually like playing ball." Royal replied.

"Well, I do; and I play very well. My dad taught me."

Royal and Leif looked at each other and shrugged.

"Okay, you can play, but we have to warn you that we kick the ball really hard."

Cherry stepped forward and kicked the ball so hard, it flew over both boys.

Royal and Leif's eyes followed the ball that was bouncing away from them.

Royal put his head down ashamed.

"I'll go get it."

Royal, Leif and Cherry were playing ball when another girl came along. She was curved like Leif, but YELLOW.

"Hi guys! What are you playing?" She asked.

Royal, Leif, and Cherry stopped playing and stared at her.

"Who are you?" Royal said.

"My name is Amber. I live on the other side of town. I saw you all and thought you might need another player."

Leif stared at Amber.

Amber stared at Leif.

"Are there more yellow curved lines on the other side of town?" Leif asked.

"No. I only know of a Blue curved family there."

"Wow," Cherry said as she looked at each of her new friends, "this is so cool. I never knew there were so many different lines."

"Yes, and we all like to play ball." Royal shouted.

"So can I play with you guys?"
Amber asked again.

"Of course, you can!"

Leif replied.

The group began to play all together.

A while later, the group saw two figures walking towards them. They didn't look familiar to any of them.

"Who are they?" asked Amber.

Royal shrugged and said, "I don't know. I've never seen them before."

Suddenly, these two "V" shapes came running,

"Can we play! Can we play!" they shouted excitedly.

The group stared at the two "V" shapes with their mouths open.

"Look how rude they are. They're just staring at us."

The PINK one said.

"HA!" laughed the PURPLE one, "They're not rude. They're shocked.

You guys have never seen "V" lines before, have you?" The purple one asked.

"Well...I... googled about them once." Amber said.

"My mom said that V lines were extinct." Leif shared.

"Well, here we are right in front of you!" the Purple one announced,

"My name is Mauve, and this is my sister Rose. We are V- lines!"

He said proudly.

The group continued to stare in awe.

Royal broke the silence first, "We were playing a game with my ball. Do you want to play with us?"

Rose and Mauve looked at each other, "YES!"

Rose and Mauve shouted excitedly.

The group kicked the ball around as new friends.

They played together all afternoon, laughing, and sharing stories about themselves.

It was a great day, and they all went home learning more about their world and their new friends!!

Other books written by Jessie

The Sun Prince

There was a Sun Prince who was always happy.

So why were his people trying to make him sad?

A sweet story about how our intentions can affect others.

Look for other stories coming soon by Jessie

Happy Reading!

Manufactured by Amazon.ca
Bolton, ON

29868248R00021